This is Jane, Jim

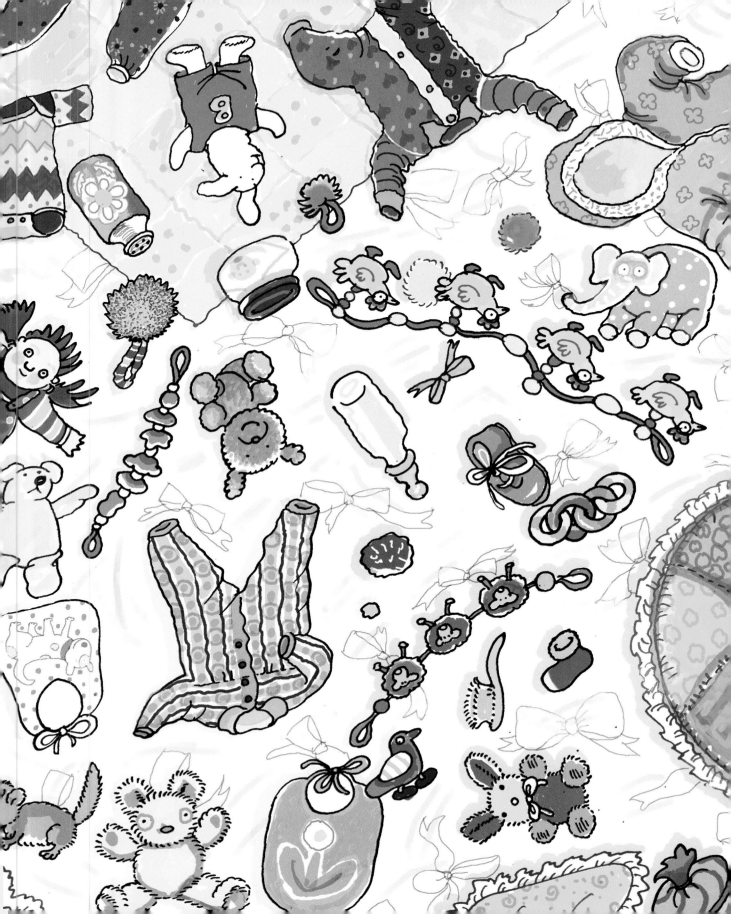

This is Jane, Jim

To Mo and Ella,
From Kaye

Love to Anne and Helen,
from Margaret

This is Jane, Jim

Kaye Umansky & Margaret Chamberlain

RED FOX

This is Jane, Jim. Our new sister.
Very small and very red.
Tiny toes and baby fingers.
Button nose and big, bald head.

She's so lovely. See her lashes?

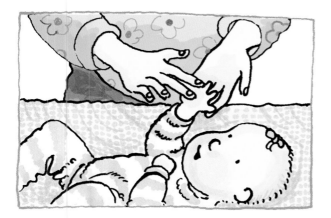

Ears like seashells, pink and small.

Mummy says that I can hold her.
Must take care she doesn't fall.

Want a go, Jim? Hold your arms out.
Keep them steady, keep them flat.

What's the matter? You don't like her?
Just what kind of talk is that?

No, we cannot send her back, Jim.
What a rotten thing to say.
Can we swap her for a hamster?
Jim, how could you! Go away.

Jim is sulking in his bedroom.
Feeling quite put out, is Jim.

Didn't want a baby sister.
No one thought of asking him.

Baby Jane gets all the cuddles
Just because she's small and new.

Poor old Jim is feeling jealous.
He wants some attention too.

What's that, Jim? You want some eggy?

Special soldiers, on a plate?

Not right now.
I've got the baby.
Sorry.
But you'll have to wait.

No, I cannot read a story.
No, I cannot draw a cow.

No, I cannot play at ghosties.
No, Jim. No, Jim. Not right now.

Jim goes stomping to his bedroom.
Crashes in and slams the door.
Climbs in bed and hugs his teddy.
No one loves him anymore.

No one cooks his favourite eggy.
No one has the time to read.
Baby Jane is taking over.
Jim is very cross indeed.

In the night, someone is crying.
Such a sad and snuffly sound.
No one is awake to hear it.
No one seems to be around.

Baby Jane lies in the moonlight,
Wailing gently in her cot.
Jim decides now is the moment
He will tell her what is what!

Jane looks up – and stops her crying.
Looks at Jim a long, long while.

Kicks her feet and waves her mittens.
Shows her gums – and starts to smile.

Reaches out to grab his finger.
Holds it very strong and tight.
Baby Jane is pleased to see him.
Jim. Admit it, Jane's all right.

In the morning,
  very early,
When the sun
  begins to peep,
Jane and Jim
  lie close together,
Gently breathing,
  fast asleep.

Later, when the sun has risen,
Jim wakes to a brand new day,
Made real nice with eggy soldiers
Brought up special, on a tray.

THIS IS JANE, JIM
A RED FOX BOOK 0 09 940929 1

First published in Great Britain in 2002 by Red Fox,
an imprint of Random House Children's Books

3 5 7 9 10 8 6 4

Papers used by Random House Children's Books are natural, recyclable products made from
wood grown in sustainable forests. The manufacturing processes conform to the
environmental regulations of the country of origin.

Red Fox Books are published by Random House Children's Books,
61-63 Uxbridge Road, London W5 5SA,
a division of The Random House Group Ltd,
in Australia by Random House Australia (Pty) Ltd,
20 Alfred Street, Milsons Point, Sydney, NSW 2061, Australia,
in New Zealand by Random House New Zealand Ltd,
18 Poland Road, Glenfield, Auckland 10, New Zealand,
and in South Africa by Random House (Pty) Ltd,
Endulini, 5A Jubilee Road, Parktown 2193, South Africa

THE RANDOM HOUSE GROUP Limited Reg. No. 954009
www.kidsatrandomhouse.co.uk

A CIP catalogue record for this book is available from the British Library.

Printed in China by Midas Printing Ltd

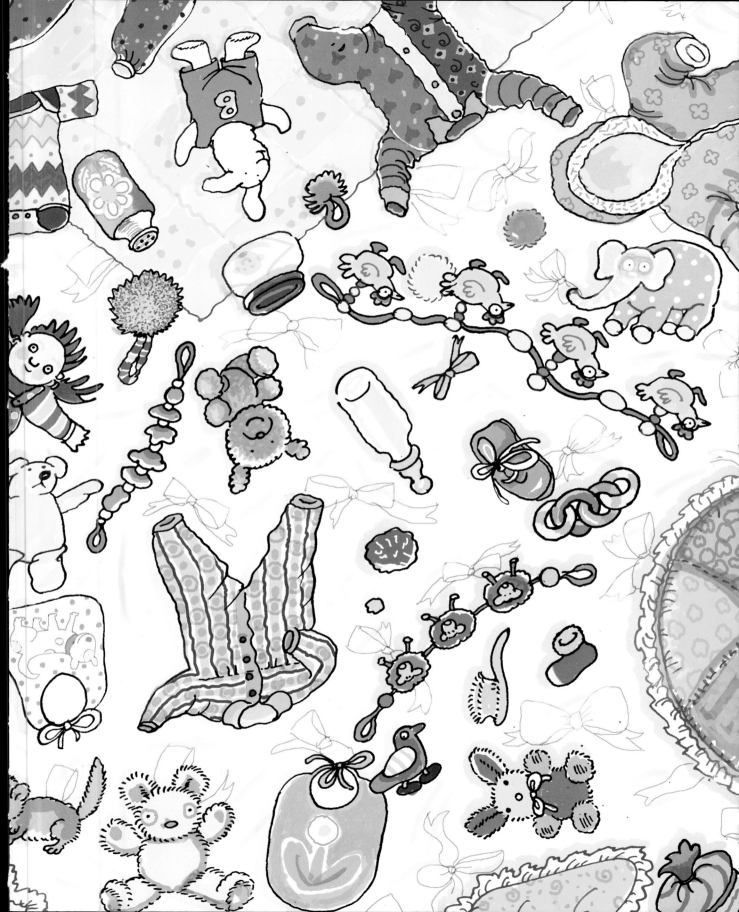

More Red Fox picture books
for you to enjoy

ELMER
by David McKee 0099697203

MUMMY LAID AN EGG
by Babette Cole 0099299119

RUNAWAY TRAIN
by Benedict Blathwayt 0099385716

DOGGER
by Shirley Hughes 009992790X

WHERE THE WILD THINGS ARE
by Maurice Sendak 0099408392

OLD BEAR
by Jane Hissey 0099265761

MISTER MAGNOLIA
by Quentin Blake 0099400421

ALFIE GETS IN FIRST
by Shirley Hughes 0099855607

OI! GET OFF OUR TRAIN
by John Burningham 009985340X

GORGEOUS
by Caroline Castle and Sam Childs 0099400766